Dear Parent:
Your child's love of reading starts here!

Every child learns to read in a different way and at his or her own speed. Some go back and forth between reading levels and read favorite books again and again. Others read through each level in order. You can help your young reader improve and become more confident by encouraging his or her own interests and abilities. From books your child reads with you to the first books he or she reads alone, there are I Can Read Books for every stage of reading:

SHARED READING
Basic language, word repetition, and whimsical illustrations, ideal for sharing with your emergent reader

BEGINNING READING
Short sentences, familiar words, and simple concepts for children eager to read on their own

READING WITH HELP
Engaging stories, longer sentences, and language play for developing readers

READING ALONE
Complex plots, challenging vocabulary, and high-interest topics for the independent reader

ADVANCED READING
Short paragraphs, chapters, and exciting themes for the perfect bridge to chapter books

I Can Read Books have introduced children to the joy of reading since 1957. Featuring award-winning authors and illustrators and a fabulous cast of beloved characters, I Can Read Books set the standard for beginning readers.

A lifetime of discovery begins with the magical words **"I Can Read!"**

Visit www.icanread.com for information
on enriching your child's reading experience.

For Eowyn and Zephyra —A.L.

I Can Read Book® is a trademark of HarperCollins Publishers.

Chicken in Mittens
Copyright © 2017 by HarperCollins Publishers
All rights reserved. Manufactured in China.
No part of this book may be used or reproduced in any manner whatsoever without written permission except in the case of brief quotations embodied in critical articles and reviews. For information address HarperCollins Children's Books, a division of HarperCollins Publishers, 195 Broadway, New York, NY 10007.
www.icanread.com

ISBN 978-0-06-236415-9 (trade bdg.)—ISBN 978-0-06-236414-2 (pbk.)

Typography by Whitney Manger

17 18 19 20 21   SCP   10 9 8 7 6 5 4 3 2 1   ❖   First Edition

CHICKEN
in
MITTENS

By Adam Lehrhaupt
Illustrated by Shahar Kober

HARPER
An Imprint of HarperCollinsPublishers

Zoey stepped out of the barn.

So did her best pig, Sam.

Fresh snow covered the farm.

"We can be explorers!" said Zoey.

"It's cold," said Sam.

"Arctic explorers!" said Zoey.

"Wear your mittens," said Clara.

Zoey and Sam wore their mittens.

"Not what I meant," said Clara.

"Where are we going?" asked Sam.

"To the North Pole!" said Zoey.

"I think it's this way."

"There's a fence," said Sam.

"And a big hill."

"And there might be yetis."

"Sounds like fun!" said Zoey.

"Let's go!"

Sam caught up to Zoey at the fence.

"Now what?" asked Sam.

"We can't go through it."

"You're right!" said Zoey.

She wiggled under.

Sam wiggled under, too.

He made it through.

But his mitten got caught.

Sam didn't notice.

He rushed to catch up.

"That's a big hill," said Sam.

"We should have a small rest."

But Zoey was already climbing.

So Sam climbed up behind her.

"It's a long way down," said Sam.

"I wish we had a sled."

"We don't have a sled," said Zoey.

"But we do have a pig!"

16

"I'm always the sled," said Sam.

"I'm better at steering," said Zoey.

YAHOO!

"Now I'm colder," said Sam.

"Where's the North Pole?"

"Let's ask the yeti," said Zoey.

"A real yeti!" said Sam.

"Do they eat pigs?"

"Probably not," said Zoey.

"Excuse me, Mr. Yeti!" called Zoey.

"Where's the North Pole?"

The yeti did not answer.

Zoey tapped the yeti's toe.

WHOOSH!

The snow slipped off.

"It's the scarecrow!" said Sam.

"He's on the North Pole!" said Zoey.

They did their happy dance.

"We made it!" said Zoey.

"We can go home," said Sam.

He blinked. "How do we get home?"

"We follow your string," said Zoey.

"Leaving it was a good idea, Sam!"

"I'm smart like that," said Sam.

"Let's go."

The friends followed Sam's string
over the hill
and back to the fence.

"There's home!" said Sam.

"Cheers!" said Zoey.

"You're a great arctic explorer."

"You too," said Sam.

"We're a perfect team."